Those Messy Hempels

Brigitte Luciani

Those Messy Hempels

Illustrated by
Vanessa Hié

Translated by J. Alison James

A Michael Neugebauer Book

North-South Books · New York · London

The Hempels were a happy-go-lucky family—but they were so messy! Usually, the Hempels didn't mind the mess, but one day they decided to bake a cake and they couldn't find the whisk. No whisk. No cake. That was a problem. So the Hempels decided to clean up.

The Hempels swirled through the kitchen like a tornado.
WHOOSH, wash the dishes. WHIST, sweep the floor.
Before they knew it, the kitchen was clean and shining!
Did they find the whisk? No!
But they did find a pillow. A pillow in the kitchen?
No. A pillow belongs in …

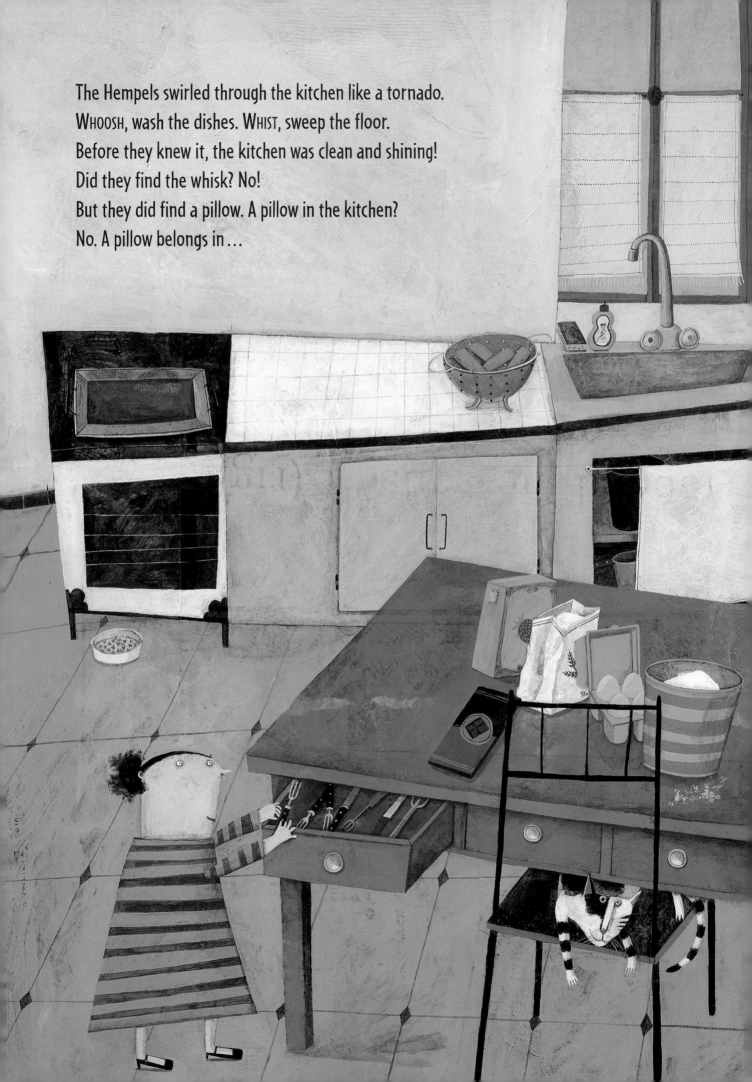

...the bedroom!
What a mess! The bedroom was a shambles. Clothes and books were scattered all over the place. The Hempels stormed in and scooped things up. Fold a shirt. Dust a shelf. Shake out the covers and make the bed.

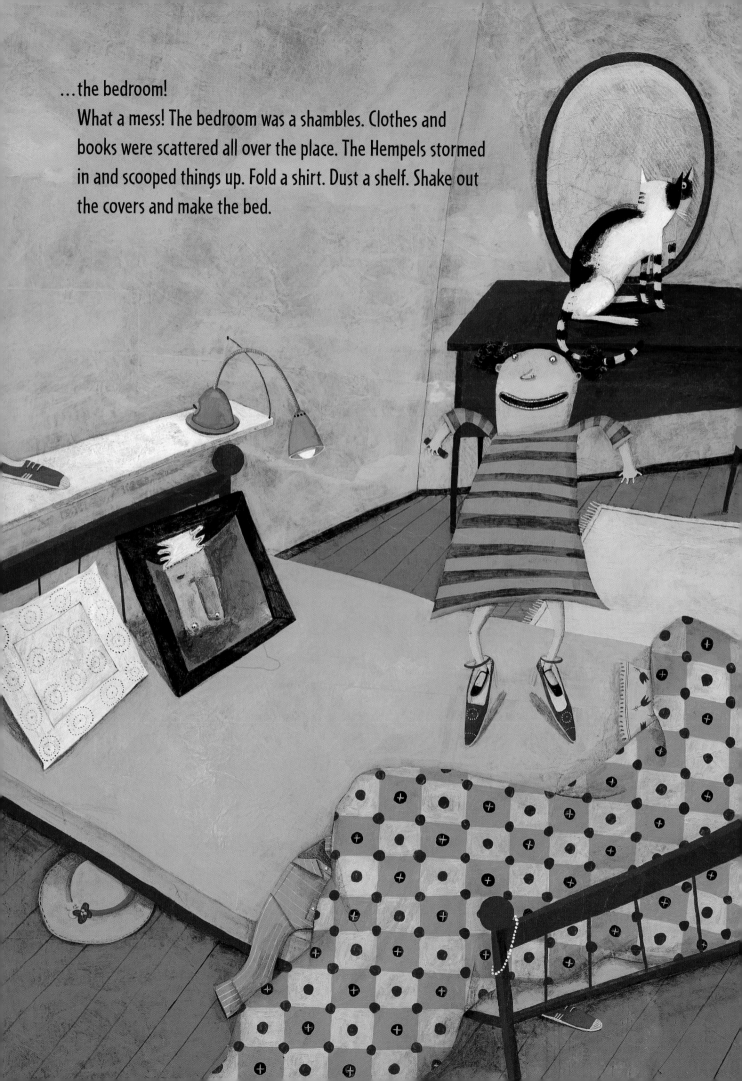

Soon the bedroom was neat and tidy.
Did they find the whisk? No!
But they did find a toothbrush. A toothbrush in the bedroom?
No. A toothbrush belongs in …

...the bathroom!
Oh my! The bathroom was loaded with laundry and the toilet paper was rolling all over the floor. The bathtub was so full of toys there was no room for water!
The Hempels cleaned up. SCRUB-SCRUB. SWISH-SWISH.

Now the bathroom sparkled like a diamond.
Did they find the whisk? No!
But they did find a rake. A rake in the bathroom?
No. A rake belongs in …

...the garden!
What a disaster! There was a pirate's fort and flowerpots lying about and a hose snaking up a tree! The Hempels went to work. CLATTER-BANG, RAKKETY-TRAKKETY, SKA-RAKE, SKA-RAKE. Even the leaves were tidied up.

There. Done.
Did they find the whisk? No!
But they did find Teddy.
A teddy bear in the garden?
No. Teddy belongs in …

…the children's room, of course.

Mother and Father took one look and collapsed on the beds.
It was SUCH a mess. Nothing was on the shelves. Everything
was on the floor.

The Hempel children took charge. They stacked and sorted
and organized, until…

"WE FOUND IT!"
Mother and Father popped up. The whisk! They'd found the whisk!

Cheering and leaping with glee,
the Hempel family ran to …

…the kitchen.
Sift the flour, melt the butter, sprinkle sugar, add some salt.
Crack the eggs and beat them with the whisk!
The Hempels made a cake.
(And the Hempels made a mess.)

Oh, what a cake! Warm and moist and melt-in-your-mouth.
The Hempels ate their cake. They didn't leave a crumb.
And did they mind about the mess?
NO!

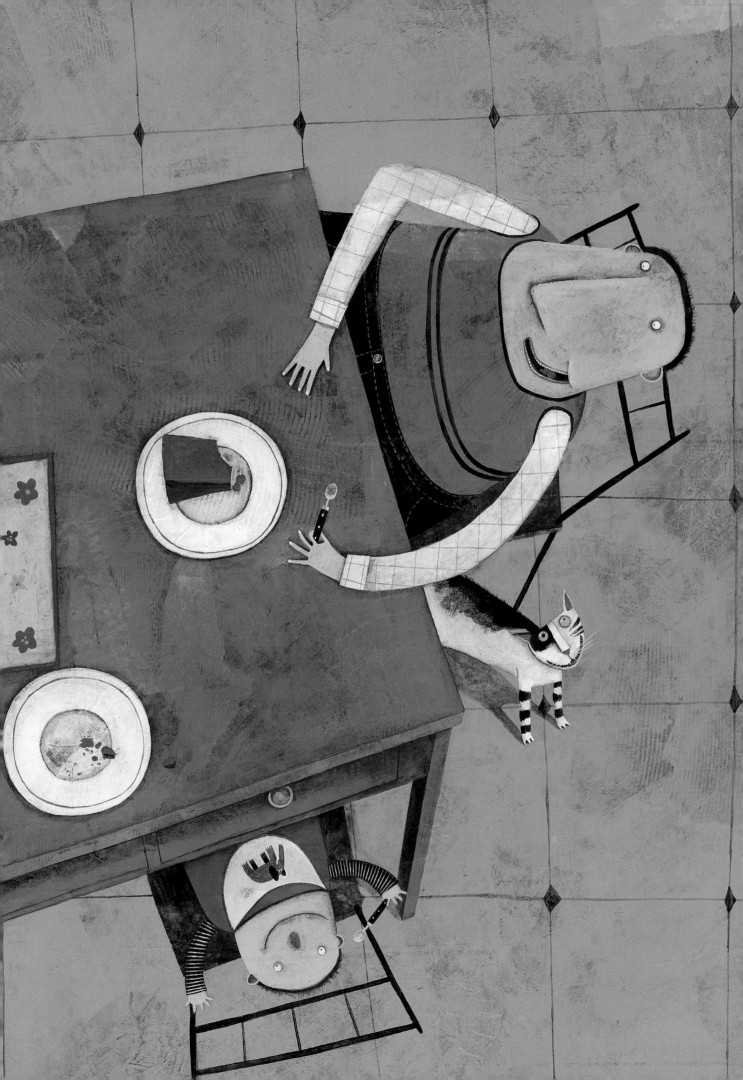

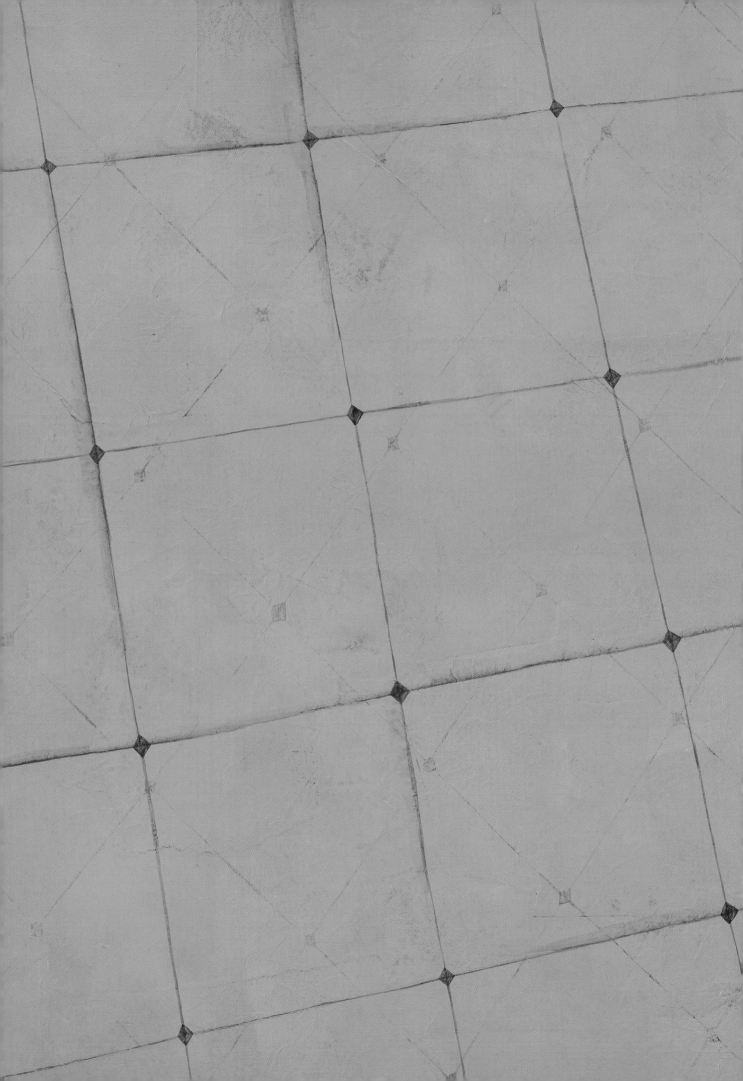

Copyright © 2004 by Michael Neugebauer Verlag,
an imprint of Nord-Süd Verlag AG, Gossau Zürich, Switzerland
First published in Switzerland under the title DIE HEMPELS RÄUMEN AUF!
English translation copyright © 2004 by North-South Books Inc., New York

First published in the United States, Great Britain, Canada, Australia, and New Zealand
in 2004 by North-South Books, an imprint of Nord-Süd Verlag AG, Gossau Zürich, Switzerland.

Distributed in the United States by North-South Books Inc., New York.

Library of Congress Cataloging-in-Publication Data is available.
A CIP catalogue record for this book is available from The British Library.
ISBN 0-7358-1909-2 (trade edition) 10 9 8 7 6 5 4 3 2 1
ISBN 0-7358-1910-6 (library edition) 10 9 8 7 6 5 4 3 2 1
Printed in Italy

For more information about our books, and the authors and artists
who create them, visit our web site: www.northsouth.com